## "Don't even blink your eyes, cousin.

"Those Mojave greens carry a double shot of poison in their fangs. Paw Paw, what are you waiting for?"

"I'm trying to make up my mind."

"Paw Paw!"

Bo caught a flash of Mzzz Mad as she made a leap down the steps. She grabbed up the clay flower pot and heaved it. The clay burst at Bo's feet. Startled, the Mojave green struck in midair and then raced off into the brush.

Martinka jammed his pistol into the sweat-blackened holster. "Granddaughter, you about scared the snake out of its skin."

BY SID FLEISCHMAN

*The Whipping Boy*

*The Scarebird*

*The Ghost in the Noonday Sun*

*The Midnight Horse*

*McBroom's Wonderful One-Acre Farm*

*Here Comes McBroom!*

*Mr. Mysterious & Company*

*Chancy and the Grand Rascal*

*The Ghost on Saturday Night*

*Jim Ugly*

*The 13th Floor*

*The Abracadabra Kid*

*Bandit's Moon*

*A Carnival of Animals*

# SID FLEISCHMAN

# Bo & Mzzz Mad

A Greenwillow Book

**HarperTrophy®**
*An Imprint of HarperCollinsPublishers*

Harper Trophy® is a registered trademark of HarperCollins Publishers Inc.

The text of this book is set in Walbaum.

Library of Congress Cataloging-in-Publication Data

Fleischman, Sid, (date)

  Bo and Mzzz Mad / by Sid Fleischman.

    p.    cm.

  "Greenwillow Books."

  Summary: When his father dies, Bo Gamage warily moves to the Mojave Desert home of his distant and estranged relatives, the Martinkas, and finds that "Mad" lives up to her name, Paw Paw despises him, and Aunt Juna hopes he'll help search for the gold mine that started a family feud.

  ISBN 0-06-029397-7 — ISBN 0-06-029398-5 (lib. bdg.) — ISBN 0-06-440972-4 (pbk.)

  [1. Family problems—Fiction. 2. Gold mines and mining—Fiction. 3. Orphans—Fiction. 4. Mojave Desert (Calif.)—Fiction. 5. Humorous stories.] I. Title.

PZ7.F5992 Br 2001

[Fic]—dc21

00-056198

First Harper Trophy edition, 2002

Visit us on the World Wide Web!

www.harperchildrens.com

For Susan Erickson,
librarian extraordinaire

# CONTENTS

*CHAPTER 1*

BUS STOP

The bus pulled away, leaving Bo standing alone at the windy crossroads. He looked all around for someone to meet him. There was no one in sight—nothing, in fact, but a clump of cactus and blowing sand and a snake's track in the dirt road.

But there was a homemade sign with a fading blue finger pointing toward the hills. Bo found the sign reassuring; the bus driver had let him off at the right place.

**QUEEN OF SHEBA, CALIF.**
**THATAWAY, 4 1/2 MILES**

Bo had a couple of relatives there, tenth or fifteenth cousins or something. Had they forgotten he was coming? He guessed that was just like those rattlebrained Martinkas. Bo himself was on the Gamage side of the family. His folks and the Martinkas hadn't been on speaking terms since the Stone Age, as far as he knew. Or even before.

He hung around for a while in the shade of some dusty runt of a tree. He hunkered down on his heels and listened to the lonely whistle of the wind. Then he decided he might as well leg it before he dried up and blew away like everything else he could see out here on the desert.

Bo had walked about a mile, getting drier and thirstier, when he noticed a rising cloud of chalky road dust ahead. Barreling toward him was an old Chevy pickup truck the color of Day-Glo red lipstick. On it came, rattling and squeaking and thumping like a one-man band. He had to jump out of the way before the girl at the wheel discovered there were brakes on the truck.

"Run me down, why don't you?" he yelled.

She backed up a little and hung out the window. "Trying to. You my cousin Bo? You one of them ornery Gamages? Where's your horns and your mangy tail?"

"I packed 'em there in my suitcase," he said. "Together with my pitchfork."

She was hardly much older than Bo—thirteen at the most, he thought. She was wearing big movie star sunglasses and a billed pink cap that said MAD on it.

She looked him over. "You're not as runty as I expected," she said.

"You must be one of those tobacco-spittin' Martinkas," Bo said. "You old enough to drive that thing?"

"I'm driving, ain't I?"

"I think I'll walk."

"Did I invite you to ride?"

"That's what you came out here for, isn't it?"

"Only to get a look at you, like at the zoo. I never laid eyes on an uppity Gamage before."

He matched her, look for look, as if they were dueling. From under her hat hung streaks of yellow hair. She was wearing a wrinkled T-shirt, bib overalls, and silver rings on all her fingers and thumbs.

Bo had never seen a genuine on-the-hoof Martinka before. He was kind of amazed that she was able to walk upright. He'd been brought up to believe that Martinkas were throwbacks to the woolly mammoth.

She kicked open the passenger door. "Aunt Juna said to stop what I was doing and run out here for you. Her car's getting fixed. So climb in."

"I'd sooner walk," he muttered, not wanting to give in to her.

"You'll melt in the sun, and I'll have to scrape up the mess. Get in, stupid."

Stupid to come out to this stupid desert, he thought. It looked just the place to settle down with a bad cough. His folks had left the California desert generations ago. And no wonder, he thought. You could get a sunburn just crossing the street. If you could find a street.

Bo gazed at the oasis shade of the cab. He threw his nylon backpack and old tin suitcase onto the bed of the truck and climbed onto the seat. He couldn't help noticing that the rear window had a lace curtain.

"What's your name?" he asked.

"Can't you read?"

"The word on your hat? Mad? That's not a name. That's a overheated mental state."

She gave Bo an airy look and exclaimed to the world at large, "Holy jumped-up Moses, will you listen to him? Overheated mental state! He's a talking Webster dictionary."

"I forgot. You barefoot Martinkas can't read."

"That's right," she said. "Only Greek and Latin.

You ought to hear Aunt Juna rattle it off when she gets mad."

"Is she an aunt? I didn't know I had an aunt Juna."

"You don't. She's my aunt. Did you ever cut paper dolls when you were a kid?"

"What?"

"Didn't you ever cut paper dolls?"

"Maybe," Bo said.

"Well, that's what Aunt Juna does. She's a great artist in her spare time, but she designs paper dolls. That's her job, I mean."

The girl swung the truck around and laid on the gas. When the road dropped down to cross a dry wash, the truck leaped out over the shallow cutbank and almost launched him through the window.

"Don't slow down on my account," Bo said.

"Wouldn't think of it."

He gave her a direct look. "What does Mad stand for? Madonna? Mad dog? Madagascar?"

She gave a little shrug. "Try Madeleine. Not that anyone can spell it."

"*M-a-d-e-l-e-i-n-e*," Bo muttered.

"What a show-off."

"Your aunt Juna put up the lace curtain?"

"Of course not. I did. It's my truck."

"Your truck?"

"Talk, talk, talk," she muttered impatiently. "Paw Paw gave it to me. What else do you want to know?"

"Who's Paw Paw?"

"What does it sound like? Cornmeal mush? Grandpa Charlie Martinka, that's who. My daddy's daddy. You can call him sir."

"Don't hold your breath."

"Talk, talk, talk. You're so green you don't know enough to keep your mouth shut in desert heat like this. Didn't they learn you anything in San Francisco? An open yap keeps drying out your spit. Next thing I know you'll be asking for a drink of water."

"I never touch the stuff. You wouldn't have a beer handy, would you? Ice cold?"

"Ha, as if your folks let you guzzle——" She stopped and began muttering to herself, "Oh, dumb you, Mzzz Mad. You forgot. He doesn't have any folks left. Just us nasty Martinkas."

Was that what she called herself? Mzzz Mad? It sounded like a mosquito in the air, about to attack. For someone giving survival advice, Bo noticed, Mzzz Mad ran off her mouth a lot. He gazed out through the dusty windshield at a windmill and a dying clump of palm trees rising in the distance.

"That Queen of Sheba?"

"Home, sweet home," she said, with the flicker of a smile.

"Not my kind of home."

She turned a quick, chilled look at him. "We don't chain visitors to the cactus. You can go back where you came from anytime you want, Bo Gamage."

He didn't answer. He couldn't go back. If the social workers weren't out looking for him, they soon would be. And they'd throw him into a foster home now that his dad was dead, dead, dead. Who'd think to look for Bo out here in this fried-up patch of desert?

He'd just have to put up with Mzzz Mad.

## CHAPTER 2

# GHOST TOWN

"There's a car behind us," Bo said, turning around for a better look. "Might be a cop car." It was hard to tell through curtains and all the dust the truck was kicking into the air.

The police can't be looking for me, he thought. How could they have followed me here? But the sight of a patrol car made him nervous.

Mzzz Mad looked up at the rearview mirror. "What would the law want with us?"

"Driving without a license," Bo said, trying to seem unconcerned. "Underage. I don't think they'd give you more than life."

"He's not flashing his lights, is he?"

"Not yet."

"You think I ought to stop?"

"You want my advice?" Bo asked.

"No."

"Stop."

"I was going to."

She pressed her sandal against the brake and pulled over to the edge of the road. Her bravado had fled, and he saw that she was as nervous as a moth.

They waited silently in a boiling cloud of the truck's own dust. Finally the car pulled up, all white with the roof lights of a sheriff's patrol car. Bo held his breath.

Through the gritty haze the deputy gave Mzzz Mad a hard squint. Then he let her off with a wave of the hand. He hardly seemed to notice me, Bo thought, and let himself relax. The deputy sped on past the truck and vanished behind his own kickup of dust.

"I guess he couldn't see that you are only nine years old," Bo said.

"What do you mean, nine? I'm thirteen! How old are you?"

"About the same."

"What do you mean, about?" she exclaimed.

He was a year younger than Mzzz Mad, but he

wasn't going to admit it. "Are we going to sit here and fry?"

"You call this hot? This is just a heavenly fall day out here on the Mojave. I might put on a wool sweater."

"Is that what you call this desert? The Mojave?"

"Let's hear you spell that, genius."

"*M-o-h-a-v-e.*"

"Wrong! Stay after school for the rest of your life."

After putting the gearshift back in drive, she eased the truck forward along the road. As if chastised, she drove slowly and carefully toward the oasis of rooftops and granite boulders in the distance.

As they approached up a low hill, the first thing Bo noticed was the Queen of Sheba Hotel, a rambling adobe building, two stories high and fixed with a broad awning like a wooden eyeshade. The front door stood wide open, as if the building were gasping for air.

The sheriff's car was parked in front.

Bo saw Mzzz Mad slump down, as if to vanish from sight behind the wheel. He gazed at a mixed pack of dogs trapped by the deep shade of a pepper tree. Their limp tongues hung out like red rags. Mzzz Mad took another peek and steered around to the back of the hotel. Except for the dogs and the patrol car, Bo saw no signs of life.

"What do you expect?" Mzzz Mad muttered. "It's a ghost town."

"A ghost town?"

"Not the scary kind with dead folks in white laundry who walk through walls."

"Shucks!" Bo exclaimed.

"See the Queen of Sheba mine over behind those big boulders on the hill? That was once in a movie. Then everybody packed up and left. Now there's just us."

"Who exactly is us?"

Mzzz Mad didn't bother to answer. She parked the truck behind the hotel and jumped out. After a quick look around she ran for the back steps. It was clear that she meant to make herself scarce until the law was safely gone. "Be careful of that little pot of geraniums. Aunt Juna's been trying to grow it for ages."

He felt a sharp flash of envy. How lucky this distant cousin of his was to own wheels of her own, even if she was too young to drive. If he had a truck, he wouldn't disgrace it by painting it lipstick red and hanging lace curtains on the window.

He pulled his backpack and gray tin suitcase out of the bed of the truck and followed her up the plank stairs. The suitcase felt hot as a frying pan. He got through the back door without banging into the clay pot with the sickly geranium in it.

"Aunt Juna says you're to stay in the Babylon Room. Upstairs."

She gave a quick spin on one of her toes, like a ballet dancer, darted into what must have been her bedroom, and shut the door.

Bo could hear voices from the front, from what he guessed must be the hotel lobby. He heard a woman say, "No, we haven't seen anyone out here in a week. It's out of season for us. But look around all you want."

"Yes, ma'am."

"If you stumble across a yeller-haired old man in silver spurs who looks mean enough to shoot, hold your fire. Tell Paw Paw if he's late for dinner again, I'll shoot him myself."

That must be Aunt Juna, Bo thought. He was surprised by the smile in her voice. He wondered if his mother's voice had sounded as playful as that. She had packed up long before he could remember her, traipsing off to India or Tibet or somewhere. She'd never come back.

Bo dragged his belongings up the polished wooden staircase. Checking the nameplates on the doors, he found the Babylon Room and walked in.

The room was big, with a lot of colored vases and broken clay pots on shelves, like a museum. He saw a brass bed, a long mirror on a stand, and a framed picture of palm trees. It surprised him how cool it was inside the hotel. He supposed the adobe walls must be a couple of feet thick.

The windows looked out on the front, and Bo looked out.

Along the weathered boardwalk, the deputy was peering in the windows of the abandoned stores and trying the locks, one after the other.

"He's looking for a couple of dim-witted crooks."

Bo turned and saw a young woman in leather sandals and a belt with a large Indian silver buckle. Her black hair looked about a yard long and ironed straight.

"Unpack and move yourself in," she added, with a smile. "I'm Juna Martinka. Can I call you Bo, or would you prefer Young Mr. Gamage?"

She was extending an olive branch right off, and it made him feel uneasy. If he took it, wouldn't all his Gamage ancestors start pointing their bony fingers at him? But she seemed so friendly. Finally he said, "Bo'll be fine. Why did you invite me down here?"

"We'll talk about that later. You must be dried out and thirsty. Want a beer?"

### CHAPTER 3

## BLACK GOLD

He followed Juna Martinka back downstairs to the large, square kitchen, all cool blue and white. She pulled a bottle of root beer out of the refrigerator.

He was relieved. A root beer was just what he wanted. He had been afraid she would expect him to drink down a bottle of regular beer. His father, the poet, had banished it from the house, insisting there was no poetry in fermented hops. Gamages, he assured Bo, savored only vintage white wines or tap water. When Bo had first tasted beer for himself, he could see no use in it except to show off to his friends.

"You can remove your war paint," she remarked, smiling again. She uncapped a diet Coke for herself. "The Martinkas are not going to eat you alive, you know."

"I don't know anything."

"I'm not sure I understand what started the bad feelings all those years ago. Do you?"

Bo cleared his throat. "A Martinka stole a mule from us, I think."

"Imagine all this bad blood over a dumb mule," Aunt Juna said.

"Hard to."

"Did you find something of your great-great-grandfather's to bring along? You knew he'd been a prospector out on the desert, didn't you?"

"Kind of," Bo said.

"I don't suppose you found anything about ol' Pegleg among your family's heirlooms?"

"Who?"

"Pegleg Smith. He's famous out here."

Bo shook his head. "Not in San Francisco. The only family stuff I could find is this old tin suitcase that belonged to my great-great-grandfather. There is a small box with a couple of black musket balls or something in it."

"Black musket balls! Hallelujah!"

What, he wondered, was she getting so excited about?

"And the scrap of a map, Bo? Did you find that?"

"No, ma'am," he answered. "Nothing that looks like a map."

"I was prepared for that. But there's plenty of time for all this later." She turned suddenly, facing him eye to eye. "As I wrote you, I was truly sorry to read about your daddy."

"Yes, ma'am."

"Want to talk about it?"

He didn't hesitate. "No."

If she'd read about his dad, what was there to add? The newspapers had referred to him as "the mad poet of Russian Hill," killed on his Harley motorcycle. Bo didn't want to think about him now, not out in public.

But he was beginning to feel a little easier about being in this nest of Martinkas. Aunt Juna didn't have a chip on her shoulder, like Mzzz Mad. He wondered how she'd act if she found out he was a runaway.

He said, "You must be the J. Martinka who sent me the bus ticket. I didn't know who J. Martinka was, exactly."

"I'm not really a Martinka. Paw Paw had two sons, and I married one of them. The brute took off for some wiggly cult and hasn't been seen since. I think he's on Saturn."

She didn't seem in any pain at having been abandoned. Bo didn't know what to say, so he said he was sorry.

She broke into a little smile. "Oh, lucky me. I love it out here, and Mzzz Mad—Madeleine—needs looking after. I'm teaching her ballet. She's wonderfully light on her feet."

"She seems to spin a lot," Bo said.

"We might as well get down to business, Bo. You can help Paw Paw. Charlie, that is."

"Me?

"I wonder if you know who he is." She held the cold bottle against her cheek. "Did you ever see any of those old cowboy movies with Soapy Martin and his educated horse, Euclid? They turn up on TV now and then."

Bo wasn't sure. "Maybe."

"Well, Soapy is Charlie Martinka. Of course he was young then, and long and straight as a broomstick."

"He was a movie star?"

"A star? That may be overstating it."

Bo nodded suddenly. "I think I saw one of those pictures once. His horse would count by dipping its head."

"I think Charlie was jealous of that horse. It got more fan mail than he did. But the studios stopped making westerns, and since Charlie couldn't really act, he retired to go prospecting out here. It's been the family trade, you know."

Bo nodded. He had never imagined he was related to a cowboy actor. Soapy Martin? His father had never mentioned a celebrity in the family, outside of himself. And poets were hardly on the same planet as movie actors.

Aunt Juna brushed the hair out of her eyes. "Even without a map Paw Paw made up his mind to find the long-lost Pegleg Smith gold mine. He's been on the hunt for the past twenty years. I guess you know Martinkas are stubborn as bobtailed mules."

"I've heard."

"Finding that treasure became Paw Paw's great mission. It would make him famous again. It gave him a reason to get out of bed in the morning. But now he's given up. He hardly gets out of bed. And when he walks around, he's so gloomy and bent he looks like the Tower of Pisa on legs. I'm worried about him."

"There's no map in my suitcase," Bo said with certainty.

"So you told me. But I'm prepared for that."

Bo finished his root beer, and Mzzz Mad came slinking around the doorway. She'd actually taken her hat off, he noticed, and tied her hair in a black velvet ribbon. Was she trying to appear in disguise?

"The fuzz went into the mine to look around," she said. "Who is he after?"

"Not after you," answered Aunt Juna. "You weren't driving out on the highway, were you? Paw Paw said you could drive only on our own dirt road, remember?"

"Of course I remember. San Francisco can back me up, can't you, sir? What was your name? Hobo? Bobo?"

Ignoring her sarcasm, Bo nodded. "She wasn't within a mile of the highway." If they were going to play at darts, she had made a tactical error. He had backed her up, and that would put her one down.

Aunt Juna finished her drink and glanced out the window. "Did you see Paw Paw anywhere, Maddy?"

"He can find his way home," Mzzz Mad replied. "What about the fuzz?"

"He said to keep a lookout for punks wandering around the desert."

"It's not against the law to be punks," Mzzz Mad pointed out.

"It is if you break into a house over in Twentynine Palms. They shot down a deputy sheriff, beat an old lady almost to death, and made off with a few thousand dollars she had squirreled away in mothballs."

Mzzz Mad absorbed the news silently and with some apprehension. Then she said, as if to change the subject, "I didn't know moths ate dollar bills."

"Whether they do or not," Aunt Juna replied, "the old lady must have believed it. How about lasagna for dinner? Mzzz Mad, you know the recipe. Bo, open a can of spinach, and would you mind bringing in some wood for that old stove? I've got to get back to the nineteenth century before bustles go out of fashion."

What was she talking about? The nineteenth century? Bustles? He remembered a line his father was forever quoting. Things were getting curiouser and curiouser.

Mzzz Mad was clearly relieved to see the sheriff's deputy leave town. Bo found himself alone with Mzzz Mad in the kitchen. "I'll open the spinach," she said. "The wood's out back. Don't look surprised. Haven't you ever seen a wood-burning stove?"

"Of course I have," Bo said. "Everything's up-to-date in San Francisco. We all have wood-burning stoves. There's even talk of indoor plumbing."

She almost cracked a smile, he thought, but of course she'd rather die before she'd let him catch one on her face.

"What's so special about black musket balls?" he asked suddenly.

"What do you mean, musket balls?"

"Homemade, I think. Lumpy as if they might have been shot."

She looked at him, thunderstruck. "Lumpy? You got some?"

"Yes."

"Cousin, don't you know what those black lumpy lumps might be?" She made a spin on her big toe and stopped with a wide spread of her arms. "Ta-da! Don't you Gamages know gold when you see it?"

"Gold isn't black."

"That's what old Pegleg Smith found and lost. Black gold."

"There's no such thing, Mzzz Twinkletoes," Bo replied. Gold was gold was gold. If that's what the balls were made of, his dad would have sold them off years ago to throw a party for his friends.

He went outside and paused at the bottom of the stairs to look around at the desert. The sun was going down in flames, or so he chose to see it, and shadows were stretching out like spiderwebs from the runty trees across the sand hills. *Like spiderwebs*. That was the way his dad might have seen it, Bo thought. He could almost feel his father's poet eyes flashing over him, surprised and approving. Bo began to whistle to himself.

Was there actually a lost gold mine out here? He had never heard that his great-great-grandfather had ever found one. C. C. Gamage had got rich publishing a newspaper in San Francisco, and got poor at it, too.

Bo found the woodpile, but the low hum of wings in the air stopped him. He gazed at the huge pile of granite boulders. Birds were flying out of the crevices, like ghosts escaped into the oncoming night.

He heard the rear screen door open, and there stood Mzzz Mad. "Cousin! Hope you don't mind black widows. They like to hide in the cracks in the woodpile. Shake off the wood before you bring it inside. We don't like spidery things in the house."

"What are those crazy birds?" he asked.

"Birds? What birds? You get left back a grade, cousin? Those are bats. They come out at night to hunt pesky insects. Haven't you ever seen bats before?"

"Not up close," Bo answered.

"They're harmless. Unless one bites you on the neck. Then you'll turn into a vampire."

"Spooky," Bo answered, and headed for the woodpile. He pulled off a split chunk of wood and tossed it to the ground. No startled, crawling things came tumbling out. He was grabbing another chunk when he became aware of a soft jingle of spurs.

He turned slowly and saw a tall man approaching out of the sunset. Bo could make out long yellow hair, hanging like dirty window curtains along the sides of his narrow, polished leather face. Stuck in the corner of his mouth was the stub of a cigar, burning like a fuse. Bo saw the gun belt and the glow of silver spurs.

"Who are you?" the man asked in a low, rumbling voice. "That boy Juna sent for? I told her I don't want any Gamages around here."

Bo looked into the man's eyes, deep as knotholes. So that was what a genuine, purebred Martinka looked like, he thought. Ugly as a mummy. A mummy in a big straw hat and wearing a hearing aid.

From the back steps Mzzz Mad gave a sudden shout of alarm. "Paw Paw, draw your gun! There's a Mojave green at the city boy's feet. It's coiling and looking to strike!"

Bo didn't need to be told she was talking about a rattlesnake. He could hear it for himself.

CHAPTER 4

# THE MOJAVE GREEN

The dry rattling at his feet was going so fast it had become a buzz. The hair shot up stiff as wire on Bo's neck. Coiled like a dusty green rope, the reptile was rearing back on itself and peering dead ahead.

"Better shoot it, Paw Paw!" Mzzz Mad called out. "You know how hot-tempered Mojave greens are!"

"A pity to waste a good varmint over a Gamage," Martinka said. "Tell the boy not to move. If that rattler bites him, the snake is bound to puny up and die."

Bo's instinct was to run. But he stayed frozen.

Martinka slowly drew his pistol. "That snake's a young'un. Shaking like a Mexican maraca, ain't he? Greens are born with a chip on their shoulders. I'd hate to be standing in that boy's shoes."

"Paw Paw! Do something!"

Bo heard Martinka cock his revolver, at last. But all
the old man did was talk. "Let's see what the creature
does," he remarked. "Not his fault he has to make a
living on the desert. The sun out here'll boil a snake
alive if it gets the chance. You can't blame the feller
for hiding in the shade of the back porch."

"You going to talk that reptile to death, Paw Paw?"

Martinka waved the pistol around. "Tell the stranger
not to move."

"Yes, sir," Bo whispered through clenched teeth.

"I wasn't talking to you, boy."

Mzzz Mad said, "Don't even blink your eyes,
cousin. Those Mojave greens carry a double shot of
poison in their fangs. Paw Paw, what are you waiting
for?"

"I'm trying to make up my mind."

"Paw Paw!"

Bo caught a flash of Mzzz Mad as she made a leap
down the steps. She grabbed up the clay flower pot
and heaved it. The clay burst at Bo's feet. Startled, the
Mojave green struck in midair and then raced off into
the brush.

Martinka jammed his pistol into the sweat-blackened holster. "Granddaughter, you about scared the snake out of its skin."

That loony old Martinka, Bo thought! He was ready to let the rattler sink its fangs into me because I'm a Gamage! Well, Gamages can hate back.

It was only when sweat began to drip off the end of Bo's nose that he realized how much moisture had been scared out of him. He was embarrassed to let Mzzz Mad see how spooked he had been. Slowly wiping his face with his sleeve, he used the time to steady his voice. Then he shrugged and said, "I've seen bigger snakes."

"Where? In the zoo?" Mzzz Mad answered in a huff. "Don't go bad-mouthing a Mojave green. Inch for inch, they're as bad as bad gets. I just about saved your life, but don't thank me."

"Thanks," Bo said offhandedly, as if only to defy her. But he did mean it. Thanks.

She ignored him. "Paw Paw, don't go wandering off. We're about to fix dinner."

He took a couple of slow sucks on his cigar. Then he blew smoke as if he were a skywriter looping a message in the air. "Martinkas and Gamages don't eat at the same table."

Mzzz Mad threw him a look over her shoulder.

"Better not count on Aunt Juna to back you up on that. Not tonight."

"I'm not unpacking," Bo announced sharply, glaring at the crazy straw-hatted old man. "I'm gone."

"Tell that to Aunt Juna," Mzzz Mad declared, with a sly grin.

CHAPTER 5

# "WHERE WILL YOU GO?"

Aunt Juna made Bo sit down. Then she gave a shout up the stairs. "Charlie, dinner is hot! If you're not in your chair, I'll give your plate to the roadrunners. Even worse, I'll give it to young Gamage to eat."

But not even that prospect moved the old man to make an appearance, so Aunt Juna said to dive in. "Don't take Charlie too seriously," she added. "He has a flair for the dramatic from his old cowboy actor days."

"He wouldn't kill that snake to save my life," Bo reminded her.

"That was for show. He told you to stand still, didn't he? That was probably the best thing to do. He didn't have his glasses on, and he knew he might shoot you rather than the rattler. Pass the rolls."

Bo wasn't convinced. Maybe. Maybe not. He didn't feel comfortable in this house. "I'll clear out first thing in the morning," he declared firmly. He wasn't keen to tramp out to the highway now, at night, with creatures like that Mojave green coming out. Where he would go when a bus came along, he had no idea. But anywhere would do.

Aunt Juna ignored his declaration and passed the butter. "Mzzz Mad, did you lift the hood of the truck?"

"In a minute," said Mzzz Mad. "I was busy saving my cousin's life, remember? I'm sorry about the geranium. It's kind of sickly-looking, anyway."

"I can repot the poor thing," Aunt Juna remarked, and turned back to Bo. "After you've been here on the desert awhile, you'll learn a few tricks. Pack rats and mice love snug places to hide, and under the hood of a car is one of them. So we leave the hood up and the engine wide open at night."

Department of useless information, Bo thought. Stay here on this creepy desert? Not in a thousand years.

"Otherwise the varmints chew up the insulation on the wires," Mzzz Mad added, clacking her teeth rapidly like a cartoon squirrel. "It's pizza with pepperoni to them. The next morning—surprise—your car's dead as a dead cat."

Aunt Juna gave Mzzz Mad a pointed look. "And that truck of yours won't last the night."

"Okay, I'm going," said Mzzz Mad, and put down her fork.

Aunt Juna's glance followed her out the back door. "Unlike you, Madeleine was practically born an orphan. Up near Death Valley. She's growing up touchy."

"I noticed," Bo muttered.

"We're the sole family she remembers. And that truck is about the only thing she owns. A scowling big windstorm came along a few months ago and sand-blasted every scrap of paint. Paw Paw promised if she'd repaint the truck, she could have it. He didn't put it into words, but it was clear he was quitting on Pegleg Smith and his wretched black gold. I hope you'll change your mind and stay with us."

"No, ma'am," Bo said.

"Where will you go?"

"I've got places."

"Name one."

Bo shifted uncomfortably in his chair. Maybe he'd cross the border into Mexico. That couldn't be too far away. Those people in charge of new orphans wouldn't think to look for him in another country.

Aunt Juna didn't seem to listen to what she didn't want to hear. She smiled as if Bo had agreed to stay on. "That old tin suitcase you brought. Does it have a lining?"

He looked up, puzzled. "A lining? I guess so."

"I knew I could depend upon you, Bo!"

"No, you can't."

She gave her fingers a snap. "It might work. Hang around and watch us jump-start Charlie's life."

Bo peered at her. Why should he care what happened to that crabby old man? And was jump-starting him, whatever she meant by that, the genuine reason she had offered Bo a place to stay? He'd persuaded himself that Aunt Juna must have imagined him left standing alone at his father's funeral. She wanted to help, even if he was a Gamage. Maybe the Gamages and the Martinkas could finally shake hands. Now he wasn't so sure. He felt tricked. Even if she wasn't a genuine Martinka, she must have learned the tricky Martinka ways.

He wondered what that shabby tin suitcase had to do with anything. Well, it was awkward to lug around, and she could have it. "Could I use your phone to find out about the bus?"

Mzzz Mad came bouncing back to her chair. "A telephone? Holy jumped-up Moses! Do you see any telephone poles? Why do you think Paw Paw moved out here in the first place? To get away from city trash like that. No, cousin, if you want to be heard on the high desert, you've got to stand on your toes and howl like a coyote."

"Then I'll just wait on the highway," Bo said.

Again he heard the jingle of spurs, and a voice rumbled behind him, "Wait for what?"

Bo looked up, way up, at Charlie Martinka, now wearing horn-rimmed glasses and, to Bo's amazement, a civilized smile.

"Waiting for a bus," said Mzzz Mad. "He's kind of sore because I saved his life. How do you figure a Gamage?"

"Can't."

"Charlie," said Aunt Juna, "I got you to take off your hat when you eat. Can't I ever get you to take off those jinglebob spurs? You're noisy."

The old man took his chair across the table from Bo, chiming with every movement. "Juna said you're related to old C. C. Gamage."

"He was my great-great-grandfather," Bo answered.

"He was a cheat."

Bo fell silent, and Aunt Juna rushed in. "Have some dinner, Charlie. While it's still warm."

"That relative of yours," Martinka growled, "he stole my granddaddy's mule."

"I heard it the other way around," Bo managed to say.

"You heard wrong," Martinka said.

Bo looked at the sun-roasted old man and decided that arguing with him would be like arguing with a waterfront drunk. Let him think what he liked.

Martinka tucked a checkered napkin under his chin. "I don't suppose that great-great-granddaddy of yours was dumb enough to leave a map in plain sight."

"Anything is possible," Aunt Juna said, appearing anxious to change the subject. "Try the Greek sausage. You remember how much you liked them over at Joshua Tree last month?"

"Liked them?" muttered Martinka, his great eyebrows lowering like storm clouds over his eyes. "I'm still trying to digest them."

When Bo went up to bed, he opened the old tin suitcase and dug out the decorated tin box that held the family heirlooms. There was the familiar shaving brush with the ivory handle as yellowed as an old tooth. There were some military medals, three rough black balls, and a faded picture of his great-great-grandfather and a man with a mule between. Could that man with twisted mustaches that looked pointed enough to darn socks—could that be Martinka himself? Surely C. C. Gamage was the other one, the happily grinning man holding a book in his oversize fist.

Bo lifted out the three black balls. Could Mzzz Mad be right about them? Maybe they weren't homemade old musket balls. He weighed one in each hand. They were heavy. Heavy as lead.

Heavy as gold?

Bo took out the small Swiss Army knife that his father had given him. He began to carve away at the black coating. Like light escaping from under a door, a streak of copper appeared. He felt a thump in his chest. Copper? The black balls must be solid gold!

## CHAPTER 6

# A MAP FOR MARTINKA

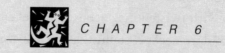

When there came a soft knock at the door, Bo knew it must be Aunt Juna. Mzzz Mad would have pounded and yelled. Martinka, he supposed, would have kicked the door in.

"So that is the old suitcase you mentioned?"

Bo nodded. He still had the knife in one hand and the three lumps of black gold in the other.

He felt the need to trust her, even if she had married a Martinka. "Are these valuable? I mean, how valuable?" he asked.

She gave a casual flutter of one hand, as if she'd seen them by the thousands. "Quite valuable. Charlie has a few just like them. That's Pegleg's famous black gold. No doubt about it. Kind of ugly, aren't they?"

I'm in luck! Bo thought. I can sell these ugly gold

lumps. Thank you, C. C. Gamage, way back a hundred years or so.

"Why'd Pegleg paint them black?" Bo asked. "To keep them a secret?"

"He didn't paint them. That black stuff is desert varnish. It's natural. Some raw chemical ages them that way. Paw Paw says it's manganese."

Bo's interest in the whole matter was exploding. He had a sudden vision of himself hiding out in Pegleg's old mine. Anytime he needed money, all he would have to do was pick up one of these black balls and cash it in.

"You said it was the *lost* Pegleg Smith mine," Bo said, pocketing the black gold. "How could anybody be dumb enough to lose a whole gold mine?"

"Easy, apparently," Aunt Juna answered, laughing. "Prospectors began looking for that mine about a hundred and fifty years ago, and still are. All I know is that Pegleg was a trapper, a moldy adventurer, and a drunken liar. He stumbled on the black gold on a hilltop somewhere. He thought the lumps were copper."

"Me, too," Bo murmured.

"It was only when he reached the coast at San Diego to sell his furs that he discovered his mistake. He claimed the hilltop was back in the Borrego

Desert south of here. That's where everyone is still looking. But they'll never find it there on the low desert."

"Why not?"

She gave a little laugh. "Because that smelly rascal on his pegleg was lying. The black gold was safe way up here two thousand feet on the high desert. On the Mojave. Two battling cousins named Martinka and Gamage were prospecting, and dumb luck, they stumbled across it. They made some sort of hand-drawn map. But one of the cousins stole their mule with the map in the saddlebag. Paw Paw believes you Gamages still have it. That's why I sent for you."

Bo felt his defenses flash up again. "The Martinkas must have it, not us! I've never laid eyes on a map."

"Maybe there never was a map, Bo." She reached into her shirt pocket and pulled out a piece of paper, folded in quarters. "But there is a map now, straight to Pegleg's black gold. See for yourself."

Bo unfolded the map. It felt very old and dry and was brown with age. He saw a trail marked in fading ink and some hills and water holes and an arrow pointing north. And an *X*.

He looked up and stared into Aunt Juna's eyes. "Then you Martinkas had it all along."

"That goofy map?" She laughed. "I made it myself. I'm not an artist for nothing, Bo dear. It looks old, doesn't it?"

He nodded slowly, baffled. What for Pete's sake was she up to?

"I got a piece of paper and soaked it in tea," she said. "That browned it nicely. Then I smudged things up and scorched the edges a little bit. This map will fool Paw Paw Charlie Martinka, don't you think?"

Bo didn't know what to think. He stared at her. "This trail and these hills and stuff are all made up?"

"Complete and beautiful fakes."

"Then what's at this *X* marks the spot?"

She laughed again and blinked her eyes. "Nothing but a restful little oasis for Charlie to rest in."

"Then what good is this map?"

"Trust me. I want you to let me hide it among your things. Maybe behind the lining of that tin suitcase of yours."

He shook his head. Was she loony? "No. Then he'll think for sure that the Gamages stole it."

"He thinks that, anyway. I'm trying to give him a reason to get up in the morning." Her eyes stayed on Bo, burrowing in. "Everyone needs a dream, Bo. Help dear old Charlie."

"He's not dear old Charlie to me."

"Of course he isn't. Then help me. Let me slip this map inside the lining of your suitcase. Once Paw Paw lays eyes on the map, he'll click his heels, give a howl, and take off like a bloodhound."

Bo turned and gazed out the window. He could just make out the huge granite boulders in the early starlight. Where were the bats now? Out hunting insects, he supposed. What made bats get out of bed in the evenings? Maybe all they dreamed about was their next insect. And what about Bo's own dreams? To do what? Not to be a fizzled-out poet like his father. Is that how the motorcycle accident had happened? Had his father's dream faded away, like Martinka's? Who dreams of becoming a busted poet?

"What do you say, Bo? I feel quite desperate. Can I tuck this map among your things?"

Why should he really care what Charlie Martinka thought about the Gamages? Bo would be leaving in the morning, anyway. A fake map. Wouldn't the joke be on Martinka? It would serve him right.

"Sure." Bo threw back the top of the suitcase. "Okay."

She investigated the green lining and found a loose corner. Carefully she began to peel it open. "Go to my room. The door is wide open. We'll need some rubber cement to repair the damage. You'll find a jar on my drawing table."

He walked down the hall to the open door. Pinned to the walls of her room were dozens of fresh drawings of paper dolls in old-fashioned clothing, as if being hung out to dry. In the center of the room stood a huge easel supporting an unfinished painting of the inside of a huge and crowded circus tent. He gazed at the plumed horses and elephants and at the painted clowns. In two spotlights a tightrope walker in black was strutting along a wire that looked about a mile high. There was no net under him. Like me, Bo thought. No net under me.

Turning away, he had to agree with Mzzz Mad. Aunt Juna was an artist. Maybe even a lot better than pretty good. And she liked circuses.

He found the jar of rubber cement on her drawing desk. He paused to look at a color snapshot pinned up: a well-tanned man standing against a dense blue sky. That couldn't be Aunt Juna's Martinka husband, he thought. Why would she pin up a picture of her ex-husband?

Bo returned to his own room with the rubber cement. Aunt Juna had the green lining of the suitcase opened up. She refolded the map and slipped it behind the lining. She used the cement sparingly. After moments to dry, no one would guess that the suitcase had been tampered with.

"Good as new." She laughed.

Good as old, he thought. Take that, Charlie Martinka.

## CHAPTER 7

# ENTER, WIZ AND HILDY

Bo was awakened in the early morning by the world coming to an end downstairs. He began to make out Mzzz Mad's voice hitting the ceiling below.

"Help, somebody! Paw Paw! Aunt Juna! Somebody stole my truck! It's gone! Is that Gamage gone, too?"

Bo pulled on his Levi's and took a couple of leaps down the stairs. "I didn't take your stupid old truck," he called out.

"Well, somebody did!"

By that time Aunt Juna was arriving in a terry cloth robe and slippers. "What do you mean, your truck is gone?"

"It's gone, as in stolen," said Mzzz Mad, now bursting into tears.

"But there's nobody out here," Aunt Juna said. "Maybe Paw Paw got up early and borrowed it."

"He's snoring thunderbolts," Mzzz Mad answered through her wet sniffles. "You know how he is lately. He turns off his hearing aid and sleeps till noon."

"You sure you set the brake? The car didn't roll back down the hill, did it?"

"Of course I set the brake!" Mzzz Mad said, deeply insulted. "I looked down the hill!"

Aunt Juna glanced out the window. "I thought I heard the dogs barking in the night. There must have been someone around. Did you hear the dogs bark?"

"Those beasts bark at every flea and kangaroo rat that comes along," Mzzz Mad cried out. "I don't know why Paw Paw brings home dogs that people turn loose out here. You'd think one of them would make a smart watchdog that would let you know when some-one is stealing your truck!"

Bo found himself feeling sorry for her. If he had a car, even an old beat-up one, he'd hate for anyone to snatch it.

Mzzz Mad caught her breath. "Wait! How about those wanted killers? Those scrungy guys the law came looking for yesterday? It could have been them!"

She was interrupted by someone knocking at the door. "I'll bet it's a prospector who saw my truck." She made a dash for the front door. "They all know it on sight."

Bo followed along behind. He might be in luck if there was someone at the door who could give him a lift out to the highway.

Instead the door opened on a girl with cotton-candy pink hair. Beside her stood a slim guy in baggy khaki pants and lizard skin cowboy boots. To Bo they looked about twenty minutes out of high school.

"Do you have a telephone?" the girl asked in an urgent voice. "We've been out camping, and we got robbed."

"Were the crooks driving a red pickup truck?" Mzzz Mad shouted out.

"I don't know," the girl said. "It was still dark. Did you see the car, Wiz?"

"It was vomit green," he said.

"Telephone? Well, no," Aunt Juna said. "We don't have service way out here."

"Not even a cell phone?" asked the girl in big-eyed disbelief.

"Not even a cell phone. But we'll get a message to the sheriff somehow."

Wiz wiped his lips. "We could use some water. Has this hotel got a restaurant? We're hungry."

Aunt Juna held open the screen door. "Come on in. We'll have breakfast going in a few minutes."

"We don't want to be no bother," said the girl.

Aunt Juna got a mesquite fire going in the stove and started the coffee. Then she left to get dressed. "Bo, fill a couple of plastic bottles with water for them to take back."

"Thanks, kid," said Wiz. "Sure smells good in here."

"It's the mesquite burning," Mzzz Mad replied. Then she slunk away, as if she had no time for these strangers with their woes. She had her own tragedy to contemplate.

Wiz looked at the views of the desert out all the windows. Finally he stretched on a kitchen chair, his lizard skin boots crossed, and gazed around the room as if he were trying to memorize the wallpaper. The coffee water began to boil.

Wiz said, "That's a mine we passed up the hill, huh? What are they hauling out of it?"

"Dirt," Bo said, resenting being questioned while Aunt Juna and Mzzz Mad were out of the room.

"No kidding? That dirt have diamonds in it, or something?"

"Dirt with dirt in it," Bo answered. "It's a fake mine. It was made for an old movie."

The girl came alive. "In a movie? Any movie stars live around here?"

"Sure, Hildy," said her boyfriend. "Didn't you see those cactuses with sunglasses?"

"Oh, ain't he funny? Ain't the Wizard of Oz funny?"

Wiz said, "What would movie stars be doing way out here? This is the boondocks, Hildy. It's the jumping-off place to nowhere."

Well, he got that right, Bo thought.

## CHAPTER 8

# THE VULTURES
# ARE COMING

With a fresh fire roaring in the stove, Aunt Juna was making pancakes when Mzzz Mad reappeared. Before taking a place at the table, she looked out the window to make sure her truck hadn't miraculously appeared.

"Look," she said, too quietly to have discovered a miracle. "Look at that, Aunt Juna."

Bo looked for himself. With bald crimson heads, huge birds came silently flying in to the ghost town rooftops and the dead palms and the hills all around.

They folded their wings like black umbrellas and perched on their big chicken feet. There must have been forty or fifty of them, Bo thought, with more flapping in. The sky was splattered with them.

"It's just like that movie!" Hildy exclaimed. "Hitchcock? Remember? That one with all the sore-head birds."

"Those are vultures," Aunt Juna said, turning from the window. "Migrating vultures."

"Is it safe to go out?" Hildy asked with genuine concern.

"They only eat dead stuff," Mzzz Mad volunteered. "You'd be surprised how many skeletons turn up out here, picked clean. City folks mostly. Vultures ain't particular."

Hildy seemed to shudder at the thought of being picked clean by vultures. Bo watched awhile longer. It looked to him as if the birds were taking their seats to watch a show.

"I wouldn't mind prospecting sometime," Wiz remarked, stretching his arms. "Imagine stubbing your toe on a rock, and it turns out to be solid gold."

Aunt Juna packed up a couple of bologna sandwiches for them to take along. Wiz dug into his boot and withdrew some hidden bills. "What do we owe you, lady?"

"Not a thing," said Aunt Juna. "You can't have anything left."

"But the dumb-dummies didn't ask me to empty my boots," said Wiz with a triumphant smile. "Here's a twenty." Then he added, "Which way is that doggone highway? I'm kind of turned around out here. Once we dig our wheels out of the sand, I'll notify the sheriff myself."

They left, and Aunt Juna handed the bill to Bo. "If you're so set on leaving us," she said, "you'll need this. It'll help with your bus fare."

CHAPTER 9

# GOOD-BYE,
# QUEEN OF SHEBA

Bo stuffed everything he cared about into his pockets and his nylon backpack and told Aunt Juna good-bye and thanks a lot. Maybe he'd send for the tin suitcase sometime. He'd need to travel light.

None of the early-morning goings-on had stirred Martinka from his bed, and Bo was glad not to have to face him again. He even muttered good-bye to Mzzz Mad and said he was glad she had thrown the clay pot at the Mojave green.

Then he left.

The vultures, lined up on the false fronts like birds in a shooting gallery, were leaving, too. They stretched out their vast wings to warm them in the morning sun and then went flap-flapping into the sky.

Bo followed the dirt road down the hill, feeling confident without asking himself what he had to be confident about. He had turned his back on his only living relatives, but at least he was free of Paw Paw Charlie Martinka.

Aunt Juna had tried to persuade Bo that Martinka's gruffness had been mostly show-off stuff and a kind of family flag-waving. Habit. Hadn't Bo Gamage arrived feeling just as hard-nosed about Martinkas? The old man would come to his senses and come around. But Bo remained unconvinced.

The morning sun began to heat his back like a flamethrower. He had hardly got half a mile when Mzzz Mad, holding down a big floppy hat, came running after him.

"I brought you a bottle of water," she said.

"I packed one."

"Only one? You'll perish. We don't have public drinking fountains every five hundred yards on the high desert, cousin. Not the way they do down below in Palm Springs."

"I'll manage," Bo said, feeling a little weary. How many times did he have to say good-bye?

In her dark movie-star sunglasses, she was now striding beside him, matching him leg for leg.

"You don't have to walk with me," he said.

"You'll probably get lost."

"How can I get lost? I'm following the road."

"Oh, you city boys are so smart," she answered. "Don't you know a wind could spring up any minute and bury the road? You'd need three county engineers and a witching rod to find it again. Or the blow sand could blind you and you'd walk in circles for days until the vultures found you and had a celebration, with party hats and noisemakers. There's one of the ugly buzzards now. Looks hungry, doesn't he?"

Bo glanced up and saw the bloody red head and wide black wings floating like driftwood on the heated air current. Wasn't there anything around Queen of Sheba, California, that didn't give you the jumping jimmies?

"And another thing—" Mzzz Mad began.

Bo interrupted. "Lay off."

"And another thing, Bo—"

"Since when did we get on a first-name basis?"

"And another thing, Bo. Paw Paw says the desert is always watching you. Watching to see you make some dumb mistake. And then it pounces on you and bleaches your bones whiter'n chalk. Look, you're already boiling like a lobster. You're bound to come down with sunstroke before we reach the highway."

"I never felt better," Bo said, even though he felt almost hot enough to burst into flames. The day was going to be a scorcher.

"There's a little shade under that scrawny smoke tree. Follow me."

Despite himself, he followed her across a dry river wash to the inviting pool of shade under a tree bent with a waterfall of thorny leaves. She held him back with her arm until she was satisfied that the coast was clear. "The poisonous gents love tree shade as much as we do."

They drank from their plastic water bottles, and Bo asked, "What did you mean about taking in lost dogs?"

"I didn't say anything about lost dogs. I said abandoned dogs. City folks from down below do that. They get tired of their hounds and turn them loose beside the road. It takes about three days in this heat for a city dog without water to go mad. Paw Paw rescued all of 'em you saw around our place."

Well, anyone would do that, Bo thought. It was only decent. That didn't make Martinka anything special.

If Bo's father had abandoned him like one of those city dogs, it was only because he hadn't had a choice. Dead was dead, no matter how it had happened. Bo wasn't going to perish on the desert. With a father who stayed up all night flipping the pages of his rhyming dictionary and slept all day, Bo had learned to care for himself. He didn't need rescuing by Charlie Martinka.

Mzzz Mad came bursting into his thoughts. "I don't suppose Aunt Juna told you she was going to get married again."

"Why should she?"

"Get married?"

"Tell me."

Mzzz Mad pulled off her hat to fan herself. "Because one of these days that park ranger from up around Death Valley is going to show up with a preacher, and she'd like to round up all the family she has for the ceremony. That includes you, I guess."

"I'm not hanging around," Bo said.

"I can see that. I'll be glad to eat your piece of the wedding cake."

"Help yourself."

"Of course, if you stick around, Aunt Juna wouldn't have to home-school me. She'd have more time for her oil painting. Cousin, if we had eight students around here, the county'd open the school over in Raindrop and send us a teacher. But we've got only seven desert-rat kids."

"And I'd make eight, I suppose."

She fanned herself with the hat as if she were Scarlett O'Hara and about to faint with surprise. "Why, indeed you would, Bo Gamage."

"Well, I'm not a desert rat," he said.

"I noticed. Well, if Aunt Juna moves out and I grow up to be ignorant as dirt, whose fault will it be?"

"Mine," he said. "All mine. And I don't intend to miss the bus talking about it."

He was out in the sun again. A moment later she was right beside him, the rings on all her fingers giving off sun sparks.

"I don't need a desert guide," he said. "So don't follow me, Mzzz Mad. If I see any blow sand, I'll cover my eyes."

"I'm not following you. I have a right to walk to the highway if I want to." She clamped her hat back on her yellow hair. "Where will you go when the bus comes?"

"Whichever way it's going."

"You could head down below to Palm Springs. And then I'll be able to write you about the funeral."

"What funeral?"

"Paw Paw's. Aunt Juna says there's a look in his eyes. He doesn't care if a Mojave green gets him or not."

"The snake'll flop over dead," Bo said, recalling Martinka's own remark about a Gamage poisoning snakes.

"You oughtn' to let Paw Paw get your goat that way," she said. "It's only because he's quit prospecting and gave me his truck and feels older'n greasewood. That's why he barked at you the way he did. Aunt Juna says if you don't have a destination rattling around inside you, you're the walking dead. Even those vultures who overnighted at our place, they got a plan in their heads. They're going to Mexico to gorge on tacos and enchiladas."

"Ha."

"Aunt Juna won't let Paw Paw quit. If he had the map to the lost Pegleg Smith mine, he'd be off, his long nose to the ground, and Mojave greens, watch out! What about you? What about me? I'm going to be a dancer in New York and London. Paris even. Aunt

Juna used to be a dancer, and she says I have good kicks and a jeté to die for. Want to see me do one right here in the sand?"

"I'll wait until you grow up."

"And what about you?"

"About me, what?"

"You want to be president at least?"

"Not me." And not a poet like my father, either, he thought. Maybe a baseball player. Poets couldn't yell at a ball game except in haiku. The trouble with poets, even when you love them, is they keep getting failing grades every day and have motorcycle accidents and leave you all alone. Well, maybe he'd be a writer when he wasn't stealing bases. He'd once started a novel. Three chapters. It was in his backpack.

"You must want something," Mzzz Mad persisted.

"Sure. To get to the highway in time for the next bus."

CHAPTER 10

# A SCENT IN THE AIR

When they reached the highway, Mzzz Mad looked both ways and said, "It could be days before a bus comes along here. You could be old enough to shave."

"I'll wait," Bo said.

"I'll wait with you."

It was dawning on him that maybe she really didn't want him to leave. It was as if her dream had really been to have someone about her own age to talk to, and even though he was a Gamage, he'd do.

But finally a bus did appear, riding the heat haze like a hydrofoil along the highway. She turned and held out her hand. "Then good-bye," she said, and added, "Of course you could change your mind. You've got about thirty seconds."

He gave her hand a shake. "Good-bye."

Then she spun around, not dancing, and started walking back up the dirt road.

Bo flagged down the bus with both arms. He climbed aboard, dug out the twenty-dollar bill, and gave it to the driver.

"How far'll that take me? Palm Springs?"

"Only if I drive backward. You're on your way to Needles."

"That's where I want to go," Bo said, and took a seat. With the air conditioning cooling his cheeks, he felt that he was returning to civilization.

But he'd hardly looked out the window when he recalled the faint, faint scent of mothballs. He took another breath, as if to test his memory. Then he jumped up and made his way forward to the driver.

"Did you smell that twenty-dollar bill I gave you?"

"This one?"

"Does it have a smell?"

The driver waved it past his nose. "Mothballs?"

"Stop the bus. Let me off, please!" Bo didn't mean to shout, but he was shouting. "I want my money back."

"Okay, okay! Take it easy, kid."

Bo snatched the bill out of the driver's gloved hand.

The moment the door swung open, he was down the steps and out in the heat again. The bus pulled away, and Bo began to shout at Mzzz Mad off in the distance.

"Wait up! Wait for me!"

He began to run, stopped to shout again, and finally caught her attention. She sat on her heels to wait for him. When he arrived, waving the twenty-dollar bill, he gave a shout. "Sniff this!"

Her arms remained moodily limp on her knees. "What did you get off the bus for? I've got better things to do than say good-bye and good-bye and good-bye all day long. Can't you make up your city-boy mind?"

"Smell it! Remember what the sheriff's deputy said? Some old lady in Twentynine Palms got beat up and robbed. She kept her money in mothballs, remember?"

"You jumped off the bus to tell me that?"

"This morning that jerky guy Wiz paid Aunt Juna with this. What do you smell?"

Mzzz Mad raised her arms and took the bill. She pressed it to her nose. She sniffed. A look of fright came into her eyes. "What if they come back?"

"We'd better warn your aunt Juna!" Bo exclaimed.

"Didn't you notice how they were eyeballing the place? Wiz looked like he planned to steal the wallpaper."

They began to run back up toward Queen of Sheba.

"Follow me, Bo!" cried Mzzz Mad. "There's a short-cut up behind the mine."

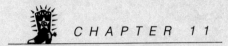

*CHAPTER 11*

# LOOKING FOR THE SPANGLES

They hurried up the road, ignoring the heat. He followed her lead as she scrambled up and over a junk pile of boulders. She made him stop in the shade of a sandy cutbank to cool off and have a drink.

"You're awfully red in the face," she said.

He slipped out of his backpack. "I'll leave this."

"That'll help. And don't open your mouth any more than you have to. It dries you out."

"You told me."

Off they went again, half running through the

midmorning heat. Scattered puddles of shade drew them like stepping-stones. "How do you know when you're getting sunstroke?" Bo muttered.

"You dizzy?"

"No."

"Then you don't have it, and shut up."

It seemed forever before Bo saw the adobe walls of the Queen of Sheba Hotel rising like a fortress in the desert.

Mzzz Mad stopped in her tracks. "See that? Big as life?"

It was hard to miss. Her lipstick red pickup truck stood parked in front of the hotel.

They hurried on. With a great huff of relief Mzzz Mad said, "Some kindly person must have found it and brought it back."

"Yeah. Some kindly person like Wiz. That sounds like him yelling."

They could hear wrecking noises, together with a hot-tempered voice, bursting from the hotel. Alarmed, Bo and Mzzz Mad bent down and crouched around until they reached the shaded side porch.

Peeking through the window, Bo saw Wiz in a whirlwind fury. He was beating the wooden drawer of the cash register into splinters.

"Lady!" he shouted. "Where do you keep your day money, eh?"

Aunt Juna was holding a scarf to her bleeding scalp. "If you miss anything," she answered, cool as ice, "I'll mail it to you. The penitentiary of your choice."

"Think you're funny?"

"I'm dead serious, Wiz."

He pulled open a drawer and emptied it on the floor. "Lady, don't think you can fool me by stringing up phony baloney about that gold mine up the hill! Movie set! Why would you hang around in the middle of Heatstroke City if you weren't digging out spangles by the ton?"

"Good question."

"Do I have to show how mean I can get? You want a letter of recommendation? Ask the cop in Twentynine Palms. Ask the old lady."

Mzzz Mad tightened her gaze and whispered, "Will you just look at Aunt Juna's head? He must have hit her!"

"Pistol-whipped her, sweetie."

The voice, a woman's voice, came from behind them.

"And you'll stick up your dainty little hands, child, or you'll get the same."

At their backs stood Hildy with a frosted-over smile. Her cotton-candy pink hair was now falling apart in long wisps. She was holding a black revolver in both hands and waving it at them.

"Both of you. Reach."

Bo flashed her a dark, uneasy look. "I don't suppose that's a stupid toy gun."

"You don't suppose right. Up."

Within moments she had snapped a handcuff onto Mzzz Mad's right wrist and Bo's left wrist. Mzzz Mad gave the cuffs a furious shake. "What do you think you're doing?"

Bo winced with the sudden pain. "Hold still! You trying to break my wrist?"

Hildy slipped the gun in the waist of her jeans. "How did you kids make yourself so scarce? Wiz told me to round you up, and I figured the vultures must have got you. The Wizard of Oz don't want you two mice out loose to run for help. He said to put police jewelry on you. Courtesy of that nice cop in Twenty-nine Palms. Now let's go inside."

Bo was sure the same thought was popping inside Mzzz Mad's head as his own: Wait for a break and run. But how fast could you run chained to somebody else?

When Hildy pushed them through the door, Wiz

stopped his ranting. A grin appeared across his unshaved jaw.

"Welcome. Howdy. Make yourselves at home. The lady here is not helping. That's dumb. You be smart. Where's the safe? Where does she stow her jewelry and gold and stuff?"

"We don't have a safe," Mzzz Mad piped up. "What would we put in it? Leftovers? I hope you have keys to these ratty handcuffs."

Wiz turned slightly. "Hildy, stupid, did you remember to take that cop's keys?"

"I think we forgot, Wiz."

"Too bad, kids. You may have to grow up that way if Hildy and I decide to make this home. I got to thinking that you don't have a telephone. Does this make a great hideout or what?"

Bo couldn't help staring at the big framed posters hung on the wall, posters of Soapy Martin, guns drawn and firing, in *Cowboy's Revenge*, and another across the lobby, eyes blazing, in *Deadly Companions*. Bo hoped that Soapy Martin in person wasn't going to sleep all day. Did he wear his gun belt to bed? Couldn't he hear something going on? Had he turned off his hearing aid?

Wiz was saying, "You folks must have more gold

than Fort Knox. Of course I don't see nothing to spend it on out here, so I suppose we'd have to skip to the big city. Guess what? That's the only way you're going to get rid of Hildy and me. So who wants to volunteer and tell the Wizard of Oz where the lady here hides her spangles?"

No one answered.

"Didn't you hear my question?"

"We heard it, Mr. Wiz," said Aunt Juna with mock respect. "The only things of value around here are a lot of paper dolls. And some books. Help yourself. Why do I have the feeling that's not what you mean by the spangles?"

"Correct," said the Wizard of Oz.

"Then you're out of luck."

"Lady, the Wiz is always in luck. Make a note of it, and don't try anything smart. 'Cause that would be dumb. Like when you bought the story we laid down about us being mugged. Put you off your guard, eh?"

"Dumb," Aunt Juna said.

Mzzz Mad raised her wrist, drawing Bo's with her, and shaking the cuffs. "Get me out of these! You must have the key!"

"Chill out and shut up," said Hildy.

Mzzz Mad ignored her. "Did they split your head open, Aunt Juna?"

"Just my scalp. Don't worry about it."

"And another thing!" Mzzz Mad went on, flashing a look at Wiz. "If it was Fort Knox around here, genius, how come we don't have gas for the stove instead of us scavenging for mesquite? And having to make our own electricity with a Sears generator? And don't have a swimming pool full of Perrier water to swim in? Answer me that?"

Bo was so busy turning an idea over and around in his head that he was hardly listening. He knew how to clear the place out. He could get rid of these pedigreed boneheads. Easy.

He lifted his hand, with Mzzz Mad's wrist jerked up with it, to catch the Wizard of Oz's attention. He spoke up in a voice as steady and self-assured as he could make it. "You want the gold? I know where the gold is. Tons of it."

Amazed, Mzzz Mad turned and peered into his eyes.

Aunt Juna lowered her black eyebrows and gave him a dismayed look.

A smile slowly blossomed on Wiz's face. "Don't scam me. Scam me, kid, and you're a dead man. The little lady'll have to drag your carcass alongside like a side of beef."

"You'll be able to scoop the gold up in both hands. All four hands," Bo said. "The only thing you need is the map."

"Hear that, Hildy?" Wiz called out.

Bo continued with so much enthusiasm that he almost believed himself. "A trail to so much gold you'll need to wear sunglasses, or it may blind you." Bo paused. "And I've got the map."

"Prove it," Wiz barked.

"Follow me."

Bo gave a small jerk on the handcuffs "You, too, Mzzz Mad."

Bewildered, she said, "You must be out of your sunstroke head."

Wiz followed Bo and called out to Hildy, "Keep your gun on the lady of the house."

Bo led the Wizard of Oz into the bedroom. The tin suitcase sat like lost luggage near the window. Bo lifted it to the bed and threw open the lid.

"Help yourself, Wiz."

"To what? That's a lot of junk."

"Pull back the lining and see what you find.

There's a map to the lost Pegleg Smith mine in there. It's been hidden in that tin suitcase for about a hundred years. Take it and hurry. No telling how many others are on the trail of Pegleg's lost gold mine."

Mzzz Mad gave Bo a yank of the handcuffs. Such a flareup of anger came over her that he could feel the heat radiating next to him.

"You rotten, no-good, double-crossing liar!" she burst out. "You skunk! You greedy, two-faced, gruesome creep! And I was beginning to tolerate you! You Gamages had the map all along! And you've let Paw Paw frazzle himself out searching for that mine!"

"Who's Paw Paw?" Wiz asked.

"None of your business!" Mzzz Mad shouted, and aimed her fury back at Bo. "You rat! You greedy, no-good bamboozler! You clunk! So that's why you turned up out here. To follow the map and claim the gold for the Gamages!"

"I don't think the little lady likes you." Wiz chuckled. He pulled a corner of the lining.

There quickly came into view not Aunt Juna's tea-stained map but three yellowed pages and a close-up photograph of a bald man. Bo was struck silent. What were these things?

Wiz shuffled through the pages. "Where's the map, kid? I warned you not to punk around with the Wizard of Oz."

Bo gazed at the pages with the spidery handwriting faded almost to invisibility. "Skip this," he said, trying to control his sudden case of the shakes. But what after all was there to be nervous about? Aunt Juna's map was right where she'd hidden it, wasn't it? "Pull open the lining at the other corner."

Aunt Juna's map fell out.

Wiz opened it up at the folds. Bo said, "Careful. You can see how old that map is. It's been hidden for a hundred years."

With a restless fingertip, Wiz followed the trail through desert and hills and dry washes to the oasis marked with an X. "Thanks, kid," he said. "I'll remember you in my will."

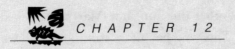

CHAPTER 12

# MARTINKA'S SPURS

They had just reached the bottom of the stairs when Bo heard the first chiming of spurs as Martinka came lumbering along the downstairs hall. Peering through his horn-rimmed glasses, he saw the trashed lobby and Aunt Juna with a bloody scarf at her head.

"What's going on out here?"

"Run for it, Paw Paw!" Mzzz Mad shouted.

Bo saw Martinka make a reach for his pistol, but there was nothing there. The old man hadn't yet buckled on his gun belt or put on his hat for the day.

"Freeze!" shouted Wiz, flashing a dark revolver. "Stand where you are."

Martinka ignored him. Striding forward on his long giraffe legs, he appeared as cool and fearless as

Gary Cooper or John Wayne or even Soapy Martin and his Educated Horse. In a flash Bo sensed that Martinka hardly cared whether Wiz shot him or not.

Wiz leveled the gun, but Martinka kicked it into the air. The younger man stumbled backward, and Martinka gave him a hard shove to the floor.

"That's not smart, scaring the wits out of my family," Martinka said, his nostrils snorting. Family? Bo wondered if that included him.

Mzzz Mad raised her arm and shook the handcuffs. "Look what they did!"

Wiz's eyes seemed to go bloodshot with anger. In a voice smart-alecky to the max, he shouted, "Hildy! Throw me your gun!"

And that, Bo thought, would be stupid to the max. Hadn't the hoodlum noticed what long arms Martinka had?

Wiz shouted again, as if to let everyone know that he was still in command. "Hildy! What you waiting for?"

She might have had her doubts about giving up the gun, but she did what Wiz commanded. She tossed him the pistol.

Wiz reached out a hand to catch it. So did Martinka.

Martinka didn't seem to hurry. He just put out his

long cowboy arm and snatched that gun right out of the air. Wiz came up empty-handed and startled. He couldn't seem to believe his own eyes.

Martinka gave him no time to review his own thick-headedness. He stuck a spur into Wiz's side. "Hold still, sonny. Otherwise I'll be obliged to sign my autograph with these jinglebob spurs."

"Hildy!" Wiz shouted.

Hildy ran. She flew out the front door. Bo saw her reach into Mzzz Mad's lipstick red pickup truck and come up with a shotgun.

She blew out a front window. "Turn him loose!" she yelled.

Without waiting for a response, she shot out another window.

"Hear? Let him go!"

"I hear!" Martinka shouted back.

He picked up Wiz like a log and sent him sailing through the broken window. The Wizard of Oz didn't glance back. Shaking off broken glass as he ran, he piled into the truck. Hildy started it up, and off they roared, kicking up a cloud of dust all the way to the highway.

Mzzz Mad began to wail. "I'll never get my truck back!"

## CHAPTER 13

# KITCHEN SURGERY

"And you!" Mzzz Mad shouted, practically in Bo's ear. "Why did you have to give him your map?"

Martinka turned, and his deep dark eyes fixed on Bo. "What map?"

"The map to the Pegleg mine, that's all!" Mzzz Mad sputtered before Bo could put a word in. But what word to put in he wasn't sure.

Bo looked at Aunt Juna, who answered for him with a slight shake of her bleeding head. Keep your mouth shut, Bo. I don't want Paw Paw to know.

"It was my cotton-picking map, wasn't it?" Bo answered. "I figured he'd run for the hills and start digging and we'd be rid of him."

"But that Pegleg Smith map rightfully belonged to Paw Paw!" Mzzz Mad protested.

"And what if Wiz started a shooting gallery in here the way he did in Twentynine Palms?"

"We'd have thought of something!"

"I got tired of waiting," Bo answered with an impatient shrug. Couldn't Mzzz Mad guess that he wasn't simple enough to give away Fort Knox with just a snap of his fingers? Didn't she smell something fishy?

"Well, you can clear out anytime you want," she snapped. "Right this minute wouldn't be too soon!"

"Right this minute will suit me fine," he answered, and dragged her by the handcuff toward the door.

She dug her heels in. "What do you think you're doing? That smarts! I'm not going anywhere with you!"

He gave the cuffs a yank. "Come on. I'll try not to notice that you're tagging along, Mzzz Siamese Twin."

"Paw Paw!" she cried out. "Can you pick this lock?"

Martinka was examining the cut in Aunt Juna's scalp. "This needs a doctor. This needs sewing together."

"It'll have to wait," Aunt Juna said. "Someone is bound to show up. Bucky Smith over in Twentynine

Palms ought to have my car about fixed. He said he'd drive it back."

"I'll sew you up myself." Martinka threw a glance over his shoulder. "Madeleine, find me a couple of large needles. And a pair of scissors. We'll do this in the kitchen. You game, Juna?"

"Have you ever done surgery before, Charlie?"

"I've sewn on a few shirt buttons."

Off they went to the kitchen. Mzzz Mad gave a sharp jerk on the handcuffs and led Bo upstairs.

At the sewing machine in Aunt Juna's room, she seemed to forget that she really wasn't talking to Bo. "He said large needles, didn't he? They'll hurt!"

"He said big ones."

"What about thread to sew her up with?"

"He must have forgotten."

She rummaged around in one of the drawers and picked out two needles and a spool of white silk thread. She handed Bo Aunt Juna's sewing scissors.

Bo jerked his head toward the snapshot of the blue sky man pinned to Aunt Juna's drawing table. "Who's the guy in all that sunshine?"

"Aunt Juna's heartthrob, not that it's any of your business. Come on."

In the kitchen, near the sink, Aunt Juna had seated

herself in a tall-backed chair. Martinka had screwed open a half-empty bottle of hydrogen peroxide and was sanitizing the wound with cotton.

The needles met his approval, and he dropped them into a saucer of the same disinfectant. Then he began washing his hands with soap.

"I won't need the thread. Now kindly scrub your hands, too, Madeleine. You'll be useful. Ready, Juna?"

"Of course not." But she said it with a smile.

Bo couldn't help being affected by her trust in Martinka and by his calm self-assurance. Bo could see that if you lived on the desert, you did for yourself.

After Mzzz Mad had scrubbed her hands, Martinka handed her a needle.

"You want me to thread it?"

"What for? We'll tie up the wound with Juna's own hair. You'll need a needle only to separate out four or five hairs together on one edge of the cut. I'll do the same on the other edge."

Martinka peered through his horn-rimmed glasses and went to work. Bo watched him take Mzzz Mad's strand of hairs and loop them together with those he had already teased out. Then he drew the wound together and knotted the hairs down tight.

He reached for the pair of scissors in Bo's free hand

and snipped the hair off a couple of inches above the knot. Then he shoved the scissors back into Bo's hand.

Mzzz Mad teased out another little clump of hair as Martinka did the same across the cut. Again he drew them together and made a tight knot. Snip. Again Mzzz Mad went to work with her needle. They repeated, knot after knot, closing up the wound as they went.

As if to keep her mind off Martinka's homemade surgery, Aunt Juna kept herself busy talking. After a moment she began to talk about Hildy. "I felt truly sorry for the girl."

Mzzz Mad scoffed. "That gun moll."

"She's sleepwalking. Put a wishbone in her hand, and she wouldn't know what to wish for. All she wants is to run with that pipsqueak Wiz. When I asked if she didn't sometimes think of becoming somebody, her expression went blank as paper. She didn't know what I was talking about. Running with Wiz was all the dream her head would hold. I told her that wasn't a dream; it was a nightmare."

"Didn't she ever see the end of *The Wizard of Oz*?" Mzzz Mad put in. "The wizard turned out to be a puffed-up fake."

Finally Martinka had the wound closed up, and the

bleeding stopped. "That should hold until we can get you to Twentynine Palms."

"Thanks, doc," Aunt Juna said. "Thanks, Mzzz Mad."

There had not been an ouch out of her. But now, without a word of warning, Martinka poured peroxide up and down the wound. It foamed up like shampoo, and Aunt Juna let out a long howl that might have reached to the highway.

Martinka began washing up at the sink, and Bo heard his name called out.

"Me?"

"Gamage. That's your name, isn't it?" Martinka asked.

"Yes, sir."

"About giving up the map to the Pegleg mine. I'll be thundered. But you did the right thing."

Bo stood astonished. Beside him Mzzz Mad shook her head as if expecting it to rattle. As if she must be hallucinating. "Paw Paw!"

"I'd have done the same thing myself. It's not worth getting killed over a glory hole in the ground. Anyway, the fun is in finding it. What was your name? Bo?"

"Bo."

Martinka cleared his throat. "You calculated you'd be able to tell the cops exactly where they'd find the punk shoveling away? Right? That was smart calculating."

And *X* marks the spot, Bo thought, provided he could remember what he had seen on Aunt Juna's map. He'd need her to refresh his memory.

"Why, Bo," said Mzzz Mad, a smile rising like dawn on her face, "I'll be thundered, too. I didn't know Gamages could be so smart."

Martinka looked at the handcuffs. "It's going to take hours to cut you apart with a dull hacksaw. But let's get started. Where's my toolbox?"

Mzzz Mad said, with a long, dismal sigh, "In the truck."

CHAPTER 14

# SANDSTORM

It was well past noon when a windstorm came up and struck the kitchen windows like buckshot. Everyone was hungry.

Mzzz Mad started fixing lunch for Aunt Juna, who was lying down with a headache, and then for herself. Bo was in her way, but she had to tag along while he spread peanut butter on a sandwich for himself.

Martinka finished covering over the broken windows with cardboard and plywood. He seemed cheered by his adventure with Wiz, as if Soapy Martin had come back to life. He made himself a plate of tacos with heavy shots of hot sauce.

Everyone waited for someone to turn up in the ghost town. Even a prospector on a mule. Someone to speed word to the highway patrol.

But the whole world seemed elsewhere, and a sand-storm blowing up wasn't going to help.

Martinka went to work trying to pick the lock on the handcuffs. He straightened out a paper clip and poked it in the small, round keyhole. Then he tried a bent wire. Finally he unscrewed a ballpoint pen and probed around with the cartridge. "I heard this is the way Harry Houdini used to escape," he said.

Mzzz Mad scoffed. "Paw Paw, they didn't have ball-point pens in those days."

"Well, if they had had 'em, that's what he would have used," Martinka said. "Hold still. I think I'm getting somewhere."

Mzzz Mad tossed a fretful glance at the ceiling. "What if Wiz is driving my truck across the border into Mexico right now? Making a getaway."

"The map to ol' Pegleg's mine will keep him on a tight leash. We'll find your truck. Just worry the wind doesn't sandblast the paint off again."

An hour later the cuff on Mzzz Mad's wrist fell open. Martinka straightened his back. "I knew Houdini used a ballpoint pen."

Mzzz Mad gave a deep sigh of relief. The Siamese twins were separated at last. But Bo was yet to be freed of the dangling manacles.

"I could go out to the highway and maybe flag someone down," Mzzz Mad said, rubbing her wrist.

"Not while this sand is blowing," Martinka replied. "We'll wait it out. The weather is slowing the punk down, too, don't forget. No hurry."

Then he set to work on Bo, trying to repeat his triumph with the first cuff. "You'd think this one used a different key," Martinka said after a while. "Let me try that paper clip again."

Bo held his arm in place on the table. He had a chance to study Martinka at close range. It came almost as a surprise that this monster of family legend appeared to be so ordinary. He breathed through his nose without snorting fire. His eyes didn't flash red. Bo found himself remembering the monster that his father had dredged up out of Lewis Carroll. Other kids could have bogeymen. A poet's son had the privilege of trembling over the wild and terrible bandersnatch.

But the bandersnatch was imaginary. Maybe the Martinka who had made him tremble was not real, either. This Martinka seemed kind of okay, taking in dogs abandoned on the desert. He'd given Mzzz Mad his truck. And hadn't he said that Bo had done the right thing in giving Wiz the map to lure him out of the hotel?

Martinka finally looked up from the handcuff. "I don't seem able to repeat my first glorious success."

Mzzz Mad said, "Let me try." After almost an hour she added, "Cousin, you may have to wear this police jewelry until it plumb wears out."

Night fell. Sand rattled the windows, and as far as Bo could see, the bats hadn't ventured out of their boulders. He was surprised to be spending another night under the Martinka roof.

Tomorrow, if the weather cleared, Bo would pick up and go. He recalled reading something about the laws of motion: A moving object wants to keep going. Sir Isaac Newton. Bo had been in motion earlier and felt a strong pull to keep going. He guessed Newton would understand.

Only when he went up to bed did he stop to pick up the old portrait hidden behind his suitcase lining. The bald man had some birthmarks across the top of his head. Who was he? A Gamage? A Martinka? Bo felt too tired and sleepy to care.

He glanced at the pages of faded writing that had surfaced together with the photo. He'd read them in the morning. He wanted to fall asleep thinking of the man in Aunt Juna's circus painting, the mile-high tightrope walker strolling along the wire without a net under him. Did he ever make it to the other side?

By morning Aunt Juna's headache was gone, and she had a fire going in the stove to make pancakes. The sand sparks at the windows had died away, and the sun was bobbing up in a rich blue sky.

"Howdy, Bo." It was Martinka himself, looking up through his horn-rimmed glasses, who first greeted him. "Good morning."

Bo didn't waste a moment on howdies and good mornings. He felt ready to explode. "I have the map to the lost Pegleg Smith mine," he exclaimed. "The real map, not that fake one. Here it is."

He placed the fading photograph of the bald man on the kitchen table.

## CHAPTER 15

# FOUND AND LOST

"You call that a map?" exclaimed Mzzz Mad. "It looks like a mug shot from the FBI! Bo, I do believe you are walking in your sleep."

"It's a map."

Aunt Juna bent closer. This was clearly a huge surprise to her.

Martinka cocked a hard look at the face of old C. C. Gamage. "Kinda shifty-eyed," he muttered. "You can see that right off."

"He looks perfectly nice to me," Aunt Juna declared.

Bo ignored Martinka's fanged remark. What had he expected the old reptile to say? A Mojave green couldn't help being poisonous. It was inherited.

Bo unfolded the sheets of paper and took a breath.

There was nothing to do but let the Martinkas in on the family secret.

"It says, 'The True Events Surrounding the Map to the Lost Pegleg Smith Gold Mine, by C. C. Gamage, in his own hand.' "

Bo could see that he had caught Martinka's attention. Even Mzzz Mad's. He stood back from the table as if he needed extra room for his arms and the sheets of paper. He read:

> "Gold makes clear-witted folks do witless things. I was reading that some ancient folks believed gold was the flesh of the gods. I doubt it. We, my cousin Henry Martinka and I, stumbled across the famous and confounded Pegleg Smith mine on the afternoon of July 13th, 1897. That gold was so blackened over and lumpy and plain ugly that the gods wouldn't have used it even on weekdays. So we had no fear that we'd bring the deities down on us if we joyfully filled our pockets. We were so rich with the stuff we could hardly walk. It wasn't in our best interests to clean out the mine and fritter our fortunes away. We could always go back for more. It was like having our own private bank."

Martinka frowned and gave out a small grunt. "I hope the young fools made a good map. Landmarks are scarce out on the desert."

Bo nodded. "Yes, sir. That started the trouble. The map.

> "We rounded up our half-wild mule, Seesaw, and loaded her with the gold we couldn't carry in our pockets. Scratched out a map and tucked that in, too. Not to mention my book of Shakespeare and Henry's wheezy old seasick green concertina. Meandering our way out of the desert, we gave a couple of lumps of black gold to a prospector friend down on his luck, Seafarin' Jim Sloat."

"Very nice of them," Aunt Juna said.

> "Not long after, that peevish mule vanished. And with our treasure map still in the saddlebag."

"Holy jumped-up Moses!" Mzzz Mad cried out.

> "My cousin Henry accused me of hiding the gold pouches and the map and then turning the mule loose with his concertina. The way he

always played that infernal squeeze-box was driving me mad, I confess. And I began to wonder if he had cut Seesaw loose with my book of Shakespeare in the saddlebag. I may have quoted the Bard oftener than necessary. With the trail to the mine still fresh in our minds, we agreed to confer and make another map. But there was hard feeling growing up between us. When we reached Los Angeles, gold still bulging our pockets, I got an idea. I remembered reading about a general planning trouble in ancient times. He ordered the head of a soldier to be shaved clean. Then he had a secret message tattooed on the bare skull. Day by day the soldier's hair grew out and concealed the message for the long, slow trip across Persia or somewhere. 'Henry,' I said impulsively, 'let's shave our heads.' And we did."

Bo could see Martinka's interest expanding at the speed of light. "Did those two nitwits have the map tattooed on their empty skulls?"

"We found a tattoo parlor on Main Street, and each had the map done up on our heads. Only we left out the $X$ mark until we could be alone. In our hotel room, with a bottle of India ink and a darning needle, I punched the $X$ mark for the mine on Henry Martinka's bare scalp. He did the same on mine. After that we drifted apart.

"Now I'll have to confess I didn't put the $X$ mark in exactly the right place on Henry's scalp."

"Cunning and tricksy!" Martinka barked out.

"The worst of it was that I was going bald as an eagle, and my hair fell out. Horrors! There was the confounded map in plain sight for all to see! I had to wear a top hat everywhere. When I went broke in the newspaper business, I returned to the Pegleg mine to make a withdrawal. But I couldn't find the place. Henry Martinka had cheated the mark, the same as I had done."

Aunt Juna shot Martinka a grin and whispered out of the side of her mouth. "Cunning and tricky."

"So the lost mine is lost again!" Mzzz Mad gasped. "And I don't think that Seesaw ran off without help.

It could have been C. C. Gamage himself who caused all the hard feeling."

Bo flashed her a triumphant smile. "And it could have been Henry Martinka, but it wasn't. My great-great-grandfather says it was Seafarin' Jim Sloat who must have crept up in the night and stole that dumb mule. When Sloat died years later, he was buried with a book of Shakespeare beside him and a green concertina. You want me to read that part?"

"I guess not," muttered Mzzz Mad, with a small, chastised shrug.

Martinka picked up the picture of C. C. Gamage's head and peered at the tattooed map. His back straightened, and his eyes began to sparkle in their deep caverns. "That looks like Little Araby Canyon to me, the way it fishhooks around. And those knobby hilltops could be the other side of Rattlesnake Dunes. That dishonest X mark can't be too far off. I'll bet I can find ol' Pegleg Smith's double lost mine!"

"I'm sure you could," Aunt Juna said gaily, as if a great burden had been lifted off her shoulders.

Suddenly Bo felt Martinka's eyes boring into him. "Where in tarnation did that first map come from? The one you gave away? What was old Gamage up to?"

Bo flicked a glance at Aunt Juna. "Hard to say, sir." That, he figured, was the honest truth.

Mzzz Mad turned to Martinka. "But this map belongs to Bo," she protested.

"We'll share out," Martinka said firmly. And then he added, almost at a shout, "Family is family."

## CHAPTER 16

# THE MILE-HIGH TIGHTROPE WALKER

There was dust traveling along the road, and Mzzz Mad was the first to notice it. "We're saved!" she called out from the window. "Someone's coming!"

It was the deputy sheriff in dusty sunglasses. He spoke right up. "You sure there haven't been any strangers hanging around here?" he asked. "They were spotted over in Raindrop."

"Was his name Wiz and her name Hildy?" Aunt Juna asked.

"We don't know their names."

"Well, you do now. And we can draw you a map exactly where to find them." Aunt Juna explained what had happened. "Would you kindly unlock the handcuffs Bo is lugging around? And could you please phone Bucky Smith over in Twentynine Palms and tell him to hurry and bring back my car? We're beginning to run out of groceries."

The deputy separated a small key on his key ring, and moments later Bo was freed. "Sir, could you give me a lift to Twentynine Palms?" he asked.

In amazement Mzzz Mad sputtered in Bo's face, "You're not leaving us!"

Bo had quickly thought things over. Martinka had said that family was family, and that was a kind of handshake; but he wasn't sure the handshake would last. If old C. C. Gamage hadn't been able to follow the fuzzy map on his head to the mine, he didn't think Martinka would. And then he'd declare the map to be nothing but another tricksy Gamage deceit, and he'd start rattling again like a Mojave green.

Bo said a quick second round of good-byes and jumped into the patrol car. He could have sworn Aunt Juna was about to burst into tears. To his surprise the jinglejangle of spurs followed him to the car. Martinka stuck his head in the window.

"I don't blame you for clearing out," he said. "I'd

have done the same thing, Bo. The old fossil who lives here was more spiteful and wrongheaded than necessary. Maybe he wanted to find out what a Gamage was made of."

"Yes, sir," Bo murmured.

"Maybe you'll come back."

"No, sir," Bo answered in a voice close to a whisper.

The sheriff's car took off down the hill. Bo saw that this time Mzzz Mad didn't attempt to follow him along the road. She turned away on the porch and vanished.

Bo could hardly believe that his voice had almost vanished, too, choked off somewhere far down in his throat. But as they passed the ledge where he'd dropped his heavy backpack the day before, he managed to say, "I need to get my backpack over there."

The patrol car sat idling while Bo looked all around the sand drifts. What had happened to his backpack? It wasn't where he had left the thing. He cast his eyes farther out. The backpack had disappeared.

"Give me another moment!" he called out.

The deputy, behind his sunglasses, didn't answer.

Bo kept moving around, trying to check his memory against the terrain.

"Did the sandstorm cover it?" shouted the deputy. "It could take you hours poking around, and I've got to hurry."

"One more second." Bo couldn't leave the backpack behind. It held everything he cared about: some pictures of him and his dad and some of his father's handwritten poems. There were even the three chapters of a novel that Bo himself had started. And he'd packed the lumps of black gold in the bottom of the backpack.

The deputy began to rev the engine. Sifting through sand with both hands, Bo now stood up and gave a defeated shout: "Never mind! Go ahead without me!"

The deputy gave him a small wave and began following his own tracks back to the highway. The road itself had largely disappeared together with Bo's backpack.

He hunkered down, sitting on his heels. A sense of being totally alone overwhelmed him. He felt like a mere speck under the sun. He watched a nervous scattering of red ants whose nest he had disturbed. What would they do now?

What would he do? He couldn't go forward, and he couldn't go back.

Or could he? The jinglejangle of Martinka's spurs had had a cheerful, friendly sound. Thoughtfully Bo got to his feet and slowly dusted himself off. Didn't that famous law of Newton's about motion also say something about another force? Another force colliding with a body in motion would stop it cold. Agreed, Bo thought.

He began to walk.

Back.

Trudging along the remnants of the dirt road, he saw Mzzz Mad come bouncing toward him, giving a twirl on her toe now and then.

"So you came to your senses! Paw Paw said you would. Hoped you would. 'That boy's family,' he said. His exact words."

He did? He said that? Holy jumped-up Moses! Bo thought. And then: "My stuff is buried in the sand."

"Of course it is!" she exclaimed. "Why, it might take weeks to find it again. Years maybe. You might as well stay with us forever."

"The foster home people up north are sure to track me down before that."

"Oh, Aunt Juna will take care of *that*," Mzzz Mad said, dismissing the matter with a snap of her ringed fingers. "But over in Raindrop the county'll start up the school, and we'll have to go, you and me. I hope you won't mind."

He could see the Queen of Sheba Hotel standing like a fortress in the desert. It looked like home. A smile got under way somewhere around his knees and rose lighter than air until it popped out like the red measles all over his face. He felt like the mile-high tightrope walker who'd reached the other side—at last.

"I guess I might as well hang around," he said. "I'll promise not to quote Shakespeare if you promise not to take up the wheezy concertina."

## CHAPTER 17

# PUBLIC NOTICE

A few mornings later Mzzz Mad got her name in the newspaper. She gave a shout and nailed the clipping to the kitchen door.

TWENTYNINE PALMS—Two teenagers on a crime spree are in handcuffs today after being surprised by sheriff's deputies at Greasewood Oasis.

Giving their names only as the Wizard of Oz and Hildy, they made a dash for their truck, a stolen red pickup belonging to Madeleine Martinka of Queen of Sheba. The vehicle, which had been left out overnight, failed to start. Rats had got under the hood and gnawed away the wiring.

# The Author's Secrets

**Where did this novel come from?**

When I stumbled across Mark Twain's line "A Kentucky feud never ends," it began to haunt me. What are more poisonous and lunatic than furies passed down through the generations? That's how wars start.

I set my story of inherited contempt not in Kentucky, where I've spent so little time, but on the California desert, where I've spent a lot.

The lost Pegleg Smith mine, with its peculiar black gold, is surely a whimsy I dreamed up. Well, no. Thomas Long Smith, a one-legged mountain man, trapper, drunk, and horse thief, claimed to have stumbled across the legendary black gold in 1828. He never found it again. Intrepid fortune hunters are still looking for it. There's a monument to Smith on the desert to the east of San Diego, where every year he is celebrated with a Pegleg Smith liars' contest.

Did thieves betrayed by mothball-scented paper money really happen? Yes. The story, an inch long, was reported in the newspapers when I was a very young writer. I have been waiting all these years for the right place to use this raw material. A short while later the spy with the tattooed head caught my eye. That curiosity was reported by the ancient Greek historian Herodotus. Writing is often a game of patience.

Finally, how about that scene where Martinka ties up a head wound using human hair? That didn't actually happen, did it? It did. Dr. Larry Garwood, my ophthalmologist, told me that his father, a small-town doctor in Canada, had once had to improvise in just such a medical emergency.

Everything else in this story I made up.

*Sid Fleischman*
*Santa Monica, California*